Daniel B. Corley

A Visit to Uncle Tom's Cabin

Daniel B. Corley

A Visit to Uncle Tom's Cabin

ISBN/EAN: 9783743395275

Manufactured in Europe, USA, Canada, Australia, Japa

Cover: Foto ©Andreas Hilbeck / pixelio.de

Manufactured and distributed by brebook publishing software
(www.brebook.com)

Daniel B. Corley

A Visit to Uncle Tom's Cabin

A Visit to Uncle Tom's Cabin.

L ATE in the month of August, 1892, I decided to make a visit to the old plantation in Natchitoches Parish, Louisiana, where I knew the original "Uncle Tom's Cabin" was still standing, just as it stood the day that the old slave died the tragic death that has been accorded him. And knowing that it was situated in the Southern portion of the parish, some twenty miles from the parish site Natchitoches, I decided to go first to that place and ascertain from the Records of Deeds and whatever else I could find, something more of the authenticity of the "story," it being my purpose, in case I could establish the fact that it was the real cabin, to make such terms as might be made with the owner of it, and then remove it to Chicago, Ill., where it would be placed upon exhibition during the World's Fair to be held in that city in 1892 and 1893.

In accordance with this plan I arrived at the old town of Natchitoches, situated on the west bank of the Red river, on the morning of the 30th day of August.

It is a singular looking town to almost any one, and especially so to a western man who is accustomed to seeing towns and cities only that are fashioned after American ideas and American fashions of the Nineteenth Century. It consists of a long, crooked row of houses fronting upon one street, and all on the

same side of the street.   This street, running up and
down the river and lying between the house-fronts
and the river banks, composes the business thorough-
fare as well as the approach to or from the place.
The steamboats in olden times would land anywhere
along this street that was convenient to put off or
take on their cargoes.   It is about forty feet wide
and as crooked as the original meandering of that
notoriously meandering river was at the time the town
was founded.   One could tell at a glance that he was
neither in Damascus nor upon the "street" called
"straight," for Damascus has a straight street and
a river, while Natchitoches can scarcely be said to
have either.

NATCHITOCHES.

I was told by the citizens of the place that the
nearest point then to the Red river from their town
was six miles away.   And this was told me by an old
man with an emphasis, impressing me with the idea
that he expected it would return at some day not far distant.   Whether he was correct, and that Red river
will come home to that town and people in the sweet-
bye-and-bye or not, I can not tell.   But for the pres-

ent, let me assure you that the town fronts upon a dry river bed. The houses are altogether of the old Southern style, one story, with heavy columned porticoes in front, while the people there take great delight in telling you that the town is the second oldest town in America.

RIVER BED IN FRONT OF NATCHITOCHES.

Shortly after my arrival, I called upon the clerk of the parish at the courthouse, whom I found to be a very estimable gentleman and possessed of the information I was in search of. He told me at once that the Legree plantation was situated in the lower portion of the parish, and that while the name "Legree" had been given to the public as the cruel slave-holder in the story of "Uncle Tom's Cabin," that in reality his name was Robert McAlpin. He further gave it as his opinion that the fictitious name "Legree" was used by the authoress of "Uncle Tom's Cabin" to prevent him, Robert McAlpin, from laying a suit for slander or defamation of character against her if he should choose to do so.

The clerk also gave me a kind of abstract of the tract of land upon which the "cabin" stood. He said that it was granted by the government to Richard McAlpin, who lived at that time, he thought, some-where in New England; that he never came out to that country at all, and that after his death his nephew, Robert McAlpin, fell heir to a portion of the tract of land and came forward and settled upon it, and after-ward bought up the interest his brothers and sisters had in it, and shortly became sole owner of it. There were 4,800 acres originally in the grant and that he, Robert McAlpin, alias "Simon Legree," lived there until his death, which occurred in 1852, at which time J. B. Chopin, the father of the present owner, bought it at administrator's sale. After the death of J. B. Chopin the tract was subdivided among his children, and that the old negro cabins and McAlpin's residence fell to his son, L. Chopin, the present owner. The records of his office show these facts.

It was in this office that I was introduced to the district attorney of that district by the parish clerk, who proved to be a brother-in-law of Mr. Chopin, the present owner of the "cabin." From these gentlemen I learned the fact that Mr. Chopin was in town at the time and that he had happened to the griev-ous loss of Mrs. Chopin, who had recently died. Though as yet he had not been seen outside of his residence. Instantly I felt at a loss as to the course to be pursued by me. I had gone six hundred miles ex-pressly to see the gentleman, only to find upon my arrival, of his late misfortune and possibly of my not getting to see him at all.

There is something in Southern chivalry not met with in all parts of the world, which both these gentlemen instantly manifested. They assured me that I should meet Mr. Chopin, and fixed the hour at five o'clock that P. M. for that meeting, and said further that instead of it being a breach of any rule of courtesy for me to offer to see him under the circumstances, that they were glad of my coming and glad of the opportunity that I would have in the approaching interview to help them dispel the gloom then hovering over their friend. Such words so freely spoken not only relieved me from my seeming embarrassment, but put me on guard as to my Christian duty at that meeting. We met, and in a gentle way I discharged that duty that one Christian owes to another under such grief-stricken circumstances, and I did so to the best of my ability. After an interview which was neither hasty nor prolonged too long, we separated to meet again the next day.

Again we met as per agreement, when it was decided that we would visit the old plantation on the next day and make a personal inspection of the "cabin," Legree's residence, his grave and such other relics and remains of that dark and dismal time and cruel and brutal man, as might still be found in existence there. Where both he and poor Tom last saw the light of that life which, though bountifully given by heaven as a gracious gift and blessing, had proven a source of long and sore distress to the one and, I doubt not, eternal damnation to the other. Having now made all necessary arrangements for the trip of the morning, which was to culminate a desire which I had cherished from my earliest boyhood by bringing me face to face with the most romantic and historic scene of my life, I next decided to employ the intervening time in inquiring of some of the older people of the place as to what they knew of "Legree" and his conduct as a man away back in the forties and fifties.

From faces already met by me there was no doubt in my mind but that plenty such could be found who would be really more at home fifty years back than at present. Notwithstanding the well authenticated rumor that a man cannot expect an assured longevity of life in the lower Red river country, yet it is a fact that in that country one will meet and continue to meet persons, both male and female, white and black, native and foreign born, whose hoary heads and deep wrinkled faces unmistakably suggest great age.

Acting upon this plan I started out along the afore-mentioned unstraightened street; nor had I proceeded very far before noticing an old man sitting at a state of rest upon a long bench under a mulberry tree in front of a saloon. Drawing near I saluted him, and taking my seat upon the other end of the bench proceeded to engage in conversation with the old gentleman. After we had exchanged a few words, which led me to the conclusion that he would engage in conversation with me, I offered him a cigar, which he politely declined saying that he had managed to live seventy years without taking up that habit and that he would not do so now. "But," said he, "Mister, I've made up at other ways and tricks all that I have ever lost by not smoking."

"Ah," said I, "it is written that 'every path hath its puddle;' and while you have not traveled all the paths of filth and vice, you have nevertheless splashed through your portion of puddles." Said he, "You bet I have."

"What is your name and nativity?" I asked.

"My name is Sam Parson and I am a native of Pennsylvania, but I have lived pretty near all my life in this here town."

"Then you must have been here among the first settlers."

"First settlers! no! no! This is an old town, so old nobody knows how old it is. It was a better town when I come to it than it is now; somehow it has not done well for the last fifty years or so."

"Have you been acquainted with it that long?"

"Yes, and longer, too. You see when I was a boy I was bound as an apprentice to a man up in Pennsylvania, and I worked with him two years and did not like him, so I run away and come South. I come to this town in 1835, and it was a good town then. You see, at that time all the emigrants that settled Western Louisana crossed this river here and afterward when the people got to going as far west as Texas, they all crossed here, too, and it made things lively."

"You must have had a good trade at that time."

"Trade! I tell you, sir, that they brought all their cotton from Houston and Austin and all Southeast Texas here on ox wagons, and sold it and bought all their supplies here. It was the liveliest town, in fact, that I ever saw, sir."

" I suppose money was plenty in those days, was it not?"

"Plentiful! You never saw the like in your life; and I made money, too. You see, I owned the ferry here, and it just kept me busy from the end of one year to another to put the folks over, and I'll tell you, Mister, they were the strangest folks you ever saw—they would just come and go. I think I have set the same families over the river as many as a dozen times, going and coming from Texas. And to tell you the truth, sir, I do not know which side of the river they stopped on at last. Some of them traveled back and forth in this way until they wore out their wagon tires."

"Well, your business must have been a profitable one to you."

"It was. I made lots of money, but then I fooled it all away somehow or other. You see, this was a great crossing. I ferried over a portion of Gen. Taylor's army here when he went to Mexico to fight the Mexicans. That was in 1846 and '47."

"Well, I suppose you lost the most of your earnings by the late war, being here and making money so early. I presume you invested in slaves and lost them like all other slave owners did."

"No, sir, I did not lose that way. I never owned but one slave in my life, and he was a good boy. I lost him when they set the niggers free, but then I do not care for that, for I intended to set him free anyhow when he got grown. I raised that boy and I never did strike him but once in all his life, and I always was sorry for that. He is the best friend I've got to-day in this world. He was powerful likely, he was. That cussed nigger trader —— heard me say when the Yankees were blowing up Vicksburg, that I believed that they would set all the niggers free. He just slapped his hands on his breeches' pocket and sez: ' I'll give you $2,200 in $20 gold pieces, right now, for your boy Jim.' I told him that I would see him in hell before he should have Jim.' So he let me alone. No, I didn't invest my money in niggers, but I put it in houses and lots right here in this town. Why, sir, at one time I owned in this town forty houses."

"Do you not own so many to-day?"

"So many to-day? I don't own a darned one."

"Why, how happened that?"

" Don't know; they went off and got a woman and brought her here, and she laid claim to about half of this town, and she brought suit for it, and I gave a lawyer a paper to represent me in the matter which he said was a power of attorney, but it was afterward found to be a deed. And him and the woman between them somehow got all I had.

" I never seed such a time. You see, she not only got all my houses and lots, but she actually wanted me to pay rent on the lots while I had used them, just as though I had never bought and paid for them. But then I didn't do it."

"So you lost all you had by her coming in and claiming the land?"

"O, yes, of course I did. Who ever heard of a fellow beatin' a cryin' woman in a suit at court? I tell you it's all stuff to fight 'em."

" This was pretty heavy on you and I am surprised that the court divested you of your title and invested it in her, did not provide for you being paid for your improvements."

"Surprised—well, you need not be. I am a much older man than you are, and I have yet to see the first court that had a lick of sense about anything, when there was a crying woman mixed up in it."

"Well, well," said I, "you are truly a historic character and I am glad to have met you. You say you settled in this town in 1835 and that you have lived here ever since; you must have known something of the cruel slave-holder, 'Simon Legree,' who was written up in a little book called 'Uncle Tom's Cabin.' The book appeared about 1852, I believe. And the whole scene was laid on the Red river here in your parish. Do you remember such a man?"

"I guess I do, and I not only remember the man, but I remember him as the meanest man that I ever knowed in my life. Why, he lived in the lower part of this parish right on the bank of the river, and was the terror of the whole country. But say, how come that woman up North who wrote that book to get his name wrong? His name was not 'Legree,' it was old Bob Mc-Alpin. She got the house and the locality and even the circumstances, as far as I know, all correct, but she missed the name. That was old Bob McAlpin. I knew him well. He was the worst man in the whole country. That woman did not tell one-half of his meanness. He sewed up a nigger in a sack and drowned him in the river.

'His chief delight was to torture his own negroes, even unto death. And he done it as often as his hellish spirit prompted him to do it. Yes; he did live and die there, as she wrote, but he was a heap meaner man than she ever made him out to be. Oh, he was bitter, he was so severe, and then he would drink so much, and all this seemed to enrage him the more. Yes, he was an old bachelor. I knew him well; he died drunk, just as she said, and was buried there on the plantation on a hill. I think that he come to this country from one of the New England states, but I could not tell you which one. I could come nearer guessing where he went to from this country than I could where he come from, if the Bible is true."

Being satisfied with my investigation and conversation with this man as to the identifying of "Legree," the plantation and the "cabin," we turned the conversation onto living issues of a later date, and finally dropped it altogether and separated. I learned afterward that Mr. Parson had once been sheriff of the parish.

Soon, however, I found myself engaged in conversation with another old timer of that section. It was L. Charleville this time, and a merchant of Cloutier ville, La. He was a fluent talker and conversed freely with me upon the subject. He said that he knew the "Legree" of "Uncle Tom's Cabin" well, and that his name was Robert McAlpin; that he had lived right there in that section all of his life; that he had served in the Mexican war under Gen. Taylor, and in the Confederate army under Gen. Lee; that he believed Robert McAlpin was among the cruelest, if not the cruelest, slave-holder he ever knew. He had read the book of "Uncle Tom's Cabin," and said Mrs. Stowe did not tell of one-half his meanness. That he was notoriously cruel to his slaves. That at times they would despair and kill themselves.

He remembered one case in particular, where at his grandfather's sale some negroes were being sold and that Robert McAlpin bid upon one of them, whereupon the negro (a man) spoke out and said to McAlpin, "If you buy me I will kill myself before night. I will not try to live with such a man as you are." That upon such a positive statement McAlpin ceased to bid and the negro was struck off to some one else. That McAlpin died in a drunken spree in 1852 and was buried on a hill on the plantation near his residence. That he knew well where the grave was, and had seen it often.

Mr. Charleville further stated that it was his opinion that Mrs. Stowe was at Robert McAlpin's house in 1850 or '51. Anyway, he says that there was a lady there at the time and accounts for Mrs. Stowe's accu-

rate description of the place in this way. That if she
was not personally present and an eye-witness of some
of these things, that the lady who was there furnished
her with a full description of the house, etc. This latter
portion of his surmise as to its being another woman is
most likely to be a correct one, for it would be a great
strain for us to imagine for a moment that a lady of
Mrs. Stowe's refined feelings and ladylike culture would
have ever taken refuge or shelter at all under the roof
of such a man as Robert McAlpin, alias "Simon Legree."

Having now become thoroughly convinced of the fact
that the locality of the "cabin" and plantation was
correctly fixed in the lower part of the parish, I desisted
from further inquiries in that direction, and retraced
my way to my boarding-house, where, seated upon one
of the old style Southern porticoes, I spent the remainder of the day in company with the landlady, who
proved to be a lady of large experience, broad and
comprehensive views and a liberal conception. She,
too, had read "Uncle Tom's Cabin," and she, like myself, had admired the gentle Christian spirit that had
prompted its authoress while penning its pages. She
was somewhat my senior in years, yet, like myself, she
had been born and raised in the South upon a slave
plantation. Twice she had been married and twice in
succession become the mistress of large slave plantations, operated in the olden way by cruel owners and
the lash. In both of which instances she had claimed
supremacy, and forced under the muzzle of her pistol
an observance of the rules of mercy. Having been
born and raised in South Carolina, from which she im-
migrated in 1856 to Natchitoches Parish, Louisiana,
where she has resided ever since, her entire life has

been encompassed by "slave traffic" and the customs of a slave country.

Yet through it all and under it all she never lost sight of her dear Redeemer; she is glad that the negro is freed; she hopes and believes that they will ever remain so, a sentiment now general in the South.

How pleasant it is, dear sister, in our life's wanderings to meet now and then one of Christ's children, whose whole life is a strong mirror reflecting the beauties and mercies of Christianity. It is a fact, that there is a comfort found and a solace felt whenever or wherever Christ's children come together and talk freely, face to face with each other, that is never felt on other occasions. So it was in this.

On the following morning, boarding the train at Natchitoches, we soon found ourselves once more rapidly speeding away through Cypress swamps all matted and woven together with dense undergrown thickets of twisting ratan. Reaching the station of Cypress on the main line of the Texas & Pacific road on time, we were, after a short delay, transferred to the down train of that road, and again soon found ourselves under full headway to our ultimate destination.

Next we arrived at the little town of Dairy, where we were joined by Mr. Chopin, the owner of the "cabin," and his little daughter Eugenie, a beautiful girl of thirteen, an only child and a father's idol. No sooner were we seated than she began talking to me and said, "I am so glad you came. I have been wanting to go down home so long and papa just would not go with me. He has just been promising me that we will go to-morrow and to-morrow for so long."

"I should have thought, Eugenie, that you would have preferred to live in town and not care to go back to the old home so quick. How long since you were there?"

"Why," said she, "I have not been there for nearly two months, and it is such a long time, and I know they all miss me so much. When I left Aunt Maria cried and said she knew something would happen, and all her children cried, and I cried myself. They were such good negroes; they were always kind to mother and to me. I taught some of them to spell in their books and to read in the Bible, and I know that they will be so glad to see me when we get there. I wish we were there now."

By this time I had gotten my eyes fairly fixed on the child, who, with her long golden hair hanging so profusely around her neck and waving so gracefully as she turned her head to right and left in emphasizing her words, that I plainly saw before me the little "Eva" of "Uncle Tom's Cabin." Never did child slip in upon me in such unsuspecting way, and so completely fill in form, figure and speech my ideal of one of whom I had only read. I saw Eva's form and figure, I heard her spirit and speech.

We soon arrived at Chopin, our place of disembarkation, and stepping out upon the platform, something like a dozen husky, dry voices sung out at once: "Why bless my life, if dar ain't Miss Genie," and crowding around shook hands with her and took on so; and then the depot agent and the clerks from her father's store, in fact everybody rushed to meet Eugenie. One could see in a moment that though she was only a child she was the queen of that valley.

We did not halt long, however, but proceeded on our intended tour, and soon came in full view of "Uncle Tom's Cabin."

As we approached it I could not help feeling a profound and deep reverence for both the place and the "cabin." In fact, it seemed to me as if I were treading upon sacred ground, and when halting in front of the house, I must admit, that the feeling that crept over me was akin to that feeling which would have come over me, had I been approaching the tomb of some patriarch of old. It was the last earthly home and

UNCLE TOM'S CABIN.

place of "Tom," the chosen instrument of Almighty God for showing to this world the evil of one man enslaving another. It always did seem to me, but when confronting the "cabin," I felt as if I knew that Tom's entire life and death had been so ordained from on high for the ultimate good of his people. That it has been used in that way no one can doubt who is familiar with his history. Our nation of people were playing total indifference to the evil of slavery, notwithstand-

2

ing the fact that that evil was creeping and crawling into all kinds of high and conspicuous places.

Notwithstanding the further fact, that our ablest and most profound statesmen were crying out at the top of their voices, warning the nation of the evil into which it was drifting, and begging them to desist from so dangerous a course. Yet with strange methodicality onward they marched, so reckless, so unmindful, so forgetful, so indifferent did the people seem that it bordered upon national oblivion.

I say that it does seem that this particular man "Tom" had been selected as the means by which and through which his people were to become liberated and freed from their bondage. Why do I say this? Let us see. Slavery was no worse at the time of his death than it was fifty years before. The slave was not treated any worse at the time of his death than they were at any given period of time during their entire bondage in the United States, and they were held in all, in bondage in the United States, 216 years. He was not the first slave that had been put upon a block and sold to a nigger trader for the highest bid, and then hand-cuffed and forced away from children, wife and all that could be near or dear to him forever. He was not the first or only slave that was ever tied and whipped to death in the country. Such incidents and events as these were almost daily occurrences in some part of the United States and had been for over 200 years. Yet the people at the North and the opponents of slavery did neither stop nor offer to stop it. But when "Uncle Tom" came to his death there was a murmur begun that widened and deepened and spread all through and through this nation. Nor did it stop there, for the historian in speaking of it says that, "The story of 'Uncle Tom's Cabin' has no parallel in the literature of any age. That in a short time there was nearly half a million copies sold in this country and a considerably larger number in England. It was translated into every language in Europe and into Arabic and Armenian. It was dramatized and acted in nearly every theater in the world." Chosen means by the same God by which that work should be done.

The combined nations of the world at once dauntingly arrayed themselves in opposition to slavery. The fight began and was waged in the United States, and ere the battle clash ceased to resound, the shackles that had bound the negro of America so long were broken; nor did the work stop here. All Europe freed all of its slaves; the South Sea Islands likewise began the work of liberating their slaves, and practically speaking, at one fell stroke the slaves of the world were liberated.

We are told that Moses was chosen as the means by which the children of Israel should be liberated from their bondage, after having served their cruel masters for 430 years. That after that was done he died and was buried. "But no man knoweth of his sepulcher until this day." Likewise we are told by the historian of Tom that "there is no monument to mark the last resting-place of our friend; he needs none. His Lord knows where he lies, and will raise him up immortal to appear with Him when He shall appear in His glory."

Add to this the soul-stirring strains of that familiar song, "God moves in a mysterious way His wonders to perform," and you will have all of the lenses through which I have looked to be convinced that Tom was made the chosen means for the liberation of his brethren, and that through him the colored slaves of the world have, like the children of Israel through Moses, been led to their respective happy lands of Canaan. Freedom in thought, freedom in utterance, freedom in action; hence my feeling a profound reverence for the place where these divine manifestations have been so plainly and impressively wrought.

Approaching the door of the cabin, we noticed that it was securely fastened with hasp and staple, made in the olden times by hand. Lifting the lock from its hold, we slowly swung back the shutter upon rudely hand-made hinges that had held it in place since 1825. We entered—all was still; the black, smoked logs with here and there a two-inch auger hole bored into their inside face into which pins or pegs were once used as supports for shelves, were plainly visible. From these it could be seen that a number of these shelves once ranged around the room I looked and wondered which one of these "Tom" kept his Bible on. But which one it was, I could not tell. Yet, that it was one of this number there is no mistake.

We next cast an upward glance at the roof which appeared to be in good shape, when we consider its great age, though it was plainly visible that at places it did " let in the sunshine and the rain;' and while gazing through these apertures at the blue sky beyond, we wondered if the spirit of "Tom," still accompanied by that of the gentle "Eva" did not at times gaze down through them upon the hard bed he once occupied there—thinking that possibly it might be so At least

> " It is a beautiful belief,
> That ever round our head
> Are hovering, on angel wings,
> The spirits of the dead."

The floor was perfectly sound and all in place, save

three or four planks that were missing from the south side of the room. This vacancy extended clear across, exposing the joist below, which appeared to have been sawed. The opening in the end wall for the fire-place was all perfectly intact, the chimney having been removed many years ago, there being only a few bricks left scattered around over the hearth-site.

Oh, thought I, could a phonograph of modern build have been placed within this room when these walls were first erected, and have recorded the successive silence and sounds that have prevailed and broken forth here in the wretched ages that have passed and gone since they were first reared, what a tale it could now tell, of sighs and sobs and sorrows; of prayers and pitiful pleadings. But we will not trace this theme further; for if it were so we might hear, reproduced, sobbing sounds of a "mother as she kissed her baby—gave it laudanum—held it to her bosom while it breathed its young life away," rather than see it grow up and follow in the miserable and wretched footsteps of her degradation; and I would not now, for all the world's present wealth, have these repeated.

Noticing that the entire house was built of heart cypress, the most durable of all woods, and that the clapboards with which it had been covered were hand-riven, and of the same material and nailed on with hand-made nails, we began to feel that we were in possession of all the knowledge we were seeking, and that we were now ready for our departure. So passing out through the doorway we closed and clasped its shutter and then departed from the place. Near by stands the old overseer's house, built about the same time, though not occupied during Legree's life by a white overseer. His negro drivers, "Sambo" and "Quimbo," evidently

resided there during the time they acted in that capacity. And afterward it was occupied by Legrée's suc-
cessors, successively ever since up to the late war. It
is now occupied by an intelligent colored man and his
family. It is a part of this man's daily business to
watch and protect the "cabin" against the raids of relic
hunters. And he told me that between the combined
effort of himself and wife, his children and his dog, that
he had succeeded wonderfully well.

We will next notice a small brick building standing
between the "cabin" and Legree's residence, but near
the latter. This building has a shed in front of it and
was the kitchen built there at the time the other buildings were erected. From some unknown cause the public
has for the last fifteen years understood that this house
was "Uncle Tom's Cabin," and in consequence of this
understanding they have pretty well pulled down and
carried the shed away as relics of it.

Mr. Chopin informed me that if the traveling public
knew which was the "cabin," there would soon be none
of it left. Said he: "Jay Gould and daughters passed
here recently, and stopping their train, got out and
went to pulling and pounding away on the old kitchen
until each of them got a clapboard, splinter, brickbat
or something else to carry away with them as relics.
And the railway men generally stop their excursion
trains here, and after showing up the place every one
sails in for a piece to carry home with him; and, seeing
the danger that the "cabin" was in, I decided not to
correct the mistake. Why, there are pieces of that
kitchen now scattered all over Europe."

This building having been originally built about
twenty steps from Legree's residence and facing directly
to it, makes it now front both it and the railroad, since

the latter passes between the two. We, therefore, have
to cross over the railroad before getting to the residence, and as we do so, halt upon the track and notice
the fact that the residence is, and always was, the only
building of all the buildings ever built upon the plantation, that stands on that side of the railroad track,
leaving all the negro cabins as they then stood, or by
any subsequent arrangement, on the opposite side of it.

RAILROAD CUT IN HILL.

Immediately on passing the residence, one exten-
sion of which had to be torn away to make room for
the road, the railroad enters a deep cut through a high
hill that jets up to where that portion of the house
stood which was removed. Not missing the corner of
that portion standing there to-day more than five feet.
The hill instead of being tunneled was cut down, leaving the banks fifty-two feet high, to stand there, an
immovable landmark through all the centuries to come.
The great enterprise of surveying and building this

railway having been both begun and completed since the death of Legree, and so plainly separating his residence forever by an immovable line from all the negro and other cabins and houses on the place, forcibly impressed me as being symbolical of another line now drawn and of far greater indestructibility between his present abode and that of the poor negroes he had once so cruelly tortured there.

SOUTH END VIEW OF LEGREE'S HOUSE.

And as I was thus musing there came a deep and fearful noise, and next a train came thundering through the cut, with its engine popping and spitting and vomiting great black clouds of smoke, intermixed with steam and fire, and thundered by with great terror, as though it was some great death-angel authoritatively traveling the boundary line on the outer borders of the respective spirit lands in the great beyond, proclaiming in thunder tones, as he passed: "No crossing! No crossing this line." The coincidence of the train's approach so quickly succeeding my first meditations

of the line being drawn, caused me to shudderingly say
unto myself: Can it be that these are truly symbolical
of the man's present spiritual condition?

There we stood gazing upon the Legree residence
that was plainly marked by the ravages of time. It
stands upon a small plat of level ground about 60 yards
from the river bank, and is completely cut off and surrounded on all sides. The hill just south of it fills all
the space between the river and the railroad. The river

TRAIN PASSING LEGREE'S RESIDENCE.

on the east, the bayou on the north, and the railroad
on the west completes the circuit. Lonely, lonely spot,
thought I, now held and used as a section house by
the railroad, occupied and tenanted alone by negroes.
There it stood precisely as it did in the olden time,
upon its brick foundation, with its "two-story veranda
running all around it and supported at its outer edge
with tall brick pillars." In front of it lies the yard that

has undergone the changes mentioned in "Uncle Tom's Cabin." The "noble avenue of China-trees, whose graceful forms and ever springing foliage seemed to be the only things there that neglect could not daunt or alter —like noble spirits, so deeply rooted in goodness as to flourish and grow stronger amid discouragement and decay," still stand there with an occasional vacancy in their rows. But the survivors clearly show to this day that the above beautiful tribute was worthily bestowed.

FRONT VIEW OF LEGREE'S RESIDENCE.

Yes, they were deeply rooted in goodness, that goodness which God gave to all the world alike, but which has been and is yet so oft and so woefully perverted.

These trees have grown until they now have large trunks ranging in size from two to three feet in diameter; and while they give evidence of decay, if properly looked after and protected from fire their "graceful foliage" will enable the historians to unmistakably locate the tragically historic spot in the year 2000.   They are trees of great longevity of life.   I only hope that they may stand long, "waving their graceful boughs" merely to designate the spot that must ever be of great historic interest to the American negro, and that they will never more shade him as a manacled and fettered slave.

The "once large garden" where "some solitary exotic once reared its forsaken head," could now only be

END OF RESIDENCE SHOWING GARRET WINDOW.

located by an occasional cluster of fig bushes, whose parent stem had once stood in the fence corner of the "garden." As we looked across its abandoned and forsaken waste, the story of the bloody Nero's once burning human bodies alive as waxen ends to light his way in his drunken walks at night in his garden, recurred to us. Likewise did these words recur to us: "How would you like to be tied to a tree, and have a slow fire lit up around it; wouldn't that be pleasant—

eh, Tom?" And we wondered to ourselves if such
threats had ever been carried into execution in the
"garden," or other similar offenses, such as sewing up
a negro in a sack preparatory to drowning him in the
river, and the like. To such inquiries, however, there
can be but one general answer, and that is that, as a
rule, men of Legree's cast and character, with abso-
lutely nothing to restrain them, will execute any threat
they may make.

Casting our eyes around we next spied, high up in
the gable at the north end of the house, a small window which evidently opened into that garret in which
Cassey and Emeline found a safe seclusion, and from
which they ultimately made their escape from their
demonized master. We had no inclination to go up in
the garret, for it was ours in boyhood to know a man
who used the garret of his residence as a place to torture his negroes in by whipping and tying them up by
their thumbs and locking them up in it for days and
nights without food or drink.

In that country, at that time, there were no steam
mills and consequently the grinding of all our grain
was done on old-fashioned grist water-mills; and it was
the custom of the people to send their grain to mill on a
horse by a boy, and to send him early in the morning
so as for him to get there first that he might get his
grinding done before the headway of water, that had
accumulated the previous night in the mill-pond, gave
out.

Upon one occasion I was sent in this way early in
the morning to mill in company with an older brother,
and the road we had to travel lay right by this man's
house who was so cruel to his negroes; and as we
were passing by we noticed old Uncle Jerry, an old

negro belonging to this man, lying by the side of an ash-hopper· that stood out in front of the yard, and he was dead. A little further on we met another negro who had been out after the horses, and we, knowing that he belonged on the same place, asked him what caused Uncle Jerry's death, and how came him to be lying out there by that ash-hopper; and he said, "Mars comed home last night en he was awful drunk, en he got mad with Uncle Jerry 'bout something, en he tuck him up in the garret en beat him so much when he come down he went out there en laid down and died."

I was then very young and a small boy; in fact, both so young and small that it was the first time that I had ever gone to mill, or been permitted to ride a horse so far by myself. And had been planning in my mind what I would tell my mother when I got back about how manly I had rode and did not let my sack fall off. I had planned further that if it all went well with me in going, that on my return I would trot my horse a little, just in order to run my cup over with glorious achievements in horsemanship. But the scene of that morning so frightened me that I lost sight of all this and cried, and when I got to the mill, the miller, who was a good man, came out and made much of me and said that I was the smallest boy he had ever seen come to mill, and that I rode well, and all that kind of talk. But I could not talk to him; my feelings were so badly torn up that I tried to speak and commenced to cry again, whereupon he asked my brother what was the matter, and when he told him, though he was a good man, how he did cuss!

We soon got our grinding done and carried it home; and when we got there we rode up behind the kitchen, and Aunt Martha, a colored woman belonging to my

father, came out to help us down, and no sooner did
she see me than she began: "Lores me, what de matter
wid dis here chile; he's been crying." Just then my
mother appeared upon the scene, and before she could
speak a word of praise to me for my success she caught
on to my brother, narrating to Aunt Martha what we
had seen. I can see that smile on her face yet as it
quickly changed into a sour contempt of what she
heard, and she spoke quickly and said that she "wished
every nigger in America was set free."

After becoming somewhat composed, I told my
mother and father as best I could all about it, and
how it had frightened me and how I tried to get my
brother to turn around and come back and he would
not do it, and how afraid I was of that man who killed
the negro, and finally brought this childish conversation to a close by asking them to never send me to
mill again by that man's house. They promised me
that they would not, and they never did. My father
partially consoled my feelings by saying further "that
there ought to be something done with that man," but
that was all.

From that day to this the name of "garret" to me
has both an unpleasant sound and sight. Hence, I
did not care to go up into that one where Cassey and
Emeline had concealed themselves preparatory to their
subsequent flight from bondage.

Having now seen about all there was to be seen,
that would be of interest to us among the remaining
buildings still standing upon the old plantation, we
decided to go one step further and see the spot where
that man who played such an active part upon the theaters of the world for nearly the last half century was
laid, when they laid him out of the light of this life.

In order to do so, we have to ascend that portion of the hill just south of the residence that lies between the railroad and the river. At the mention of going to the grave of Legree, we noticed a ripple of indifference mingled with scorn as it flashed over the face of our little heroine, Eugenie. Up to this point she had led the way and manifested great interest in pointing out her little play houses at and around the residence of Legree, and told us how she used to go to Uncle Tom's cabin and play of evenings, and seemed to be delighted to show and explain all to us. But on the mention of the grave she spoke quickly and said: "Why, there is nothing up there but his grave, and who wants to see that? I don't and I don't intend to either;" and accompanying her words with an affirmative nod of her head, gracefully declined to follow us up the hill, but said she would wait and go with us out to the church when we came back.

We slowly climbed up the hill to where its top takes a ridge shape and is covered with tall trees, from every branch and limb of which hangs in great profusion long tapering bunches of greenish looking moss, about one hundred yards, to where the ridge widens out a little, and we came to the grave of Robert McAlpin, alias "Simon Legree." His remains lie there beneath a brick tomb, that was originally built to the average height, but which has by long neglect and exposure been reduced until it does not now stand more than a foot above the level. Around it and covering nearly the entire little flat mentioned are a number of other graves. These, we were told, were all the graves of negroes, many of whom he had cruelly put to death in his lifetime, he being the only white person buried there.

We stood and gazed in silence over the stillness
that lay before us, and remembering that somebody
had said, "Oh, the grave! the grave! It buries every
error, covers every defect, extinguishes every resent-
ment. From its peaceful bosom springs none but
fond regret and tender recollections." Beautiful
words, thought I, beautifully portraying a Christian
spirit. But, thought I further, how much of this was
applicable to the mound now rising before me? How

GRAVE OF ROBERT MCALPIN, ALIAS SIMON LEGREE.

much "fond regret" had ever been felt over his death?
How many "tender recollections" of him had any one
ever cherished for one moment for any good thing he
had ever done or said? And the continued silence
negatively answered, not one, not one.

Again we turned through the ever written leaves of
recollection, and again we read, "The evil that men do
lives after them. The good is oft interred with their

bones." Yes, it is true; the evil that this man did lived
after him, playing a prominent part in plunging a nation
into war, slaughtering hundreds of thousands of men
and wrecking millions more. True literally true; but
the latter part of the sentence, "the good is oft interred
with their bones." How is this? We have just said
that if he ever said or did a good thing, there is no
written or traditional evidence of it. It would, therefore, be a monstrous revolution of all written rules for
us to suppose that any good was ever buried with him
here. We felt perplexed. It was the first time in our
entire life that we had appeared for or against a man
or even over his grave, and could not in the whole
vocabulary of our existence find a single palliating sentence to pronounce in his behalf. However, finally and
without effort on our part, we decided that he had done
well when he got out of this world, and no sooner did
the thought suggest itself than we placed it to his
credit, and turned and left the loneliest looking of all
the lonesome places we have ever seen.

Retracing our steps, we soon got back down the hill
to the residence where we left Eugenie and found her
mounted upon the high steps, on the east front of the
house, with some dozen or more negro children all
around her with their eyes and mouths wide open, lis-
tening to what "Miss Genie" had to say. And she, like a
little queen, was authoritatively asking this one and that
one if they had kept up their studies in their books,
and if they minded their mothers, and when was the
preacher there last, and did they go to church and hear
him, etc. To all of which there seemed to be a common response of "Yesum."

After getting a drink of water and resting a few
moments, we decided to move on and see the little

church that Eugenie spoke of; and as we moved off
there came a shout of "Good-bye, Miss Genie; come
again fo' long," the which she promised to do. Walking along the railroad track we soon came to the trestle
bridge spanning the deep dark gulch, which passes
from a swamp into the river, down into which Cassey
and Emeline plunged on the night they passed "along
by the quarters" when "a voice called to them," and

CHURCH.

turning back in this gulch, passed by their pursuers
unnoticed to the house and concealed themselves in the
"garret."

The deep gulch passes from this swamp close to the
quarters, thence near the house of Legree, and thence
to the river. Its position upon the ground, and its
relation to both quarters and residence, is conclusive
proof that the authoress of "Uncle Tom's Cabin" either
viewed it once in person, or else got her information

from one who had made a careful survey of it. After
crossing over the bridge we turned up the gulch on the
opposite side from where the "cabin" stands, about a
hundred and fifty yards, to the little church. As we
approached it, Eugenie commenced again: "Now,
just see that little church; well, my papa gave a lease
to the ground for this church for ninety-nine years for
five cents a year, and he built the church for them
besides, and it is so nice. I love to come here to
church and see and hear the negroes shout. You see
they are all Methodists, and they do shout and carry
on so! I am so glad to see them have a church right
here so close to 'Uncle Tom's Cabin.' Old Legree
would not let his negroes have any church or books
either. I hate to read about that man, he was so fear-
fully cruel."

We assented to all our sweet Eugenie said, and as
she drifted into silence we could not help feeling and
even repeating to ourselves: O, Christ, it is finished!
Dear Saviour, in Thy name it is finished. Here in this
once lonely vale among the "lowly," where the bare
mention of Thy name or the expose even late at night
of Thy Holy Book, by the dimly-flickering rays of a
dying cabin fire, was sure to meet with severest rebukes
and rebuffs. We now see, lifting its humble head
above the ruins of time, a church, reared and dedicated
to Thee, where the "lowly" in an humble and becoming way daily worship their Creator. Here, too, upon
this historic spot, so graphically outlined as the once
isolated and far away place, where human cruelties and
tortures equaled the most barbaric practices of ancient
time, we to-day see palace cars of the finest modern
build, drawn by the mightiest and swiftest engines of
earth as they halt; whilst their owners, railway kings

of the world, walk out and gaze long and intently upon its ruins. And as their trains move on from the scene, loving sisters and friendly hands can be seen waving scarfs which seem to take up the spirit and re-echo the sentiment. Thank God! it is finished. Ay, beyond this we wonder if that watchful convoy of angels that once broke the stillness of night on the plains of Galilee with singing their hozannas of joy, have not taken up the strain further on, and chantingly wafted them into the happy Canaan, far, far away.

It was now growing late at evening, and our day's work being finished, we turned our steps toward the depot, where, after a short rest, our train hove in sight and pulling up at the place, we boarded it again for our home in Texas. At the next station, Dairy, we bade farewell to Mr. Chopin and our gentle Eugenie, and as we shook her little hand, felt that we would one day meet her again in "a land fairer than this."

Being now thoroughly satisfied as to the identity of the plantation as that of the Legree of Mrs. Stowe's narrative of "Uncle Tom's Cabin," I closed a trade with Mr. Chopin by which he gave me a lease on the cabin for the purposes of exhibiting it at the World's Fair at Chicago, and such other places as I might deem fit to exhibit it afterward. And shortly afterward I went to Chicago, where, after some time, I contracted with the Libby Prison War Museum Association for its exhibition upon their ground in that city.

Following this I soon returned to the old plantation in Louisiana after the cabin, and on the first day of December, 1892, at noon, we began the work of taking it down, with five negro men whom I had hired to help me do the work. One of these men was a carpenter, and had been living on the plantation since

1867. After the cabin was taken down, these negro men asked me if I did not think it proper for the spot to be marked in some way by which the exact locality would not be forgotten. They talked sensibly about it, too, and said that as long as the cabin was standing there, they could show it to the rising generation with exact precision. But now that it was gone, they felt that the spot would soon be tilled as the balance of the field, and the place soon be entirely forgotten.

At the time, I promised the men that I would do what I could to keep the place green in the minds of the negro race, and after due deliberation upon the matter, and further, after advising with a number of ladies in Abilene, and Fort Worth, Texas, and in St. Louis and Chicago, as to the most feasible plan to do this, have been by them advised to keep a contribution box in the cabin during its exhibition; the deposits of which are to go toward building an academy of learning on the exact spot from which the cabin was taken.

Considering this advice good and the plan a feasible one, I have decided to keep in the cabin a box, into which visitors will be allowed and even solicited to put whatever they may feel disposed to, for this purpose. A very small contribution from each one will in a few years create a fund sufficient, no doubt, for this purpose.

Rev. W. E. Penn, of Eureka Springs, Ark., once built a church at Palestine, Texas, that cost $40,000, and he done it with nickle contributions. And I think that a similar contribution on the part of the visitors to this historic house will soon create a sufficient fund to build a house for them that will be both a credit to the givers and a pleasure and profit to the poor negroes. Let us try it. It ought to be done.

It was upon this return trip after the cabin, that I learned that during the late war there had been a battle fought upon the Legree plantation. H. H. Russell, who now owns a large saw mill upon the plantation, was at the time of this battle stationed at Monette's Ferry on Red river, about two miles away. He belonged at the time to Company D, Fourth Texas Cavalry. The fight lasted only an hour or two, and was one of those fierce artillery duels which frequently occurred when both armies were on the move. The batteries of the respective forces, Federal and Confederate, occupied two hilltops about three-quarters of a mile apart, with Uncle Tom's cabin in the valley between. This caused a shower of shell and shot to fall all around it. To this day they occasionally plow up a shell near it. In taking the building down, we found a piece of the contents of a shell which had exploded over the cabin, sticking in one of the moss-covered boards. This I brought along, together with a number of shells and parts of shells that the negroes had picked up around the building in after years. These will be kept on exhibition during the time in the cabin, whenever it may be exhibited.

During this engagement there was one Confederate soldier killed near the cabin, just in the edge of the little field that now surrounds it. His name was O. J. Polly. He was from Orange, Texas. On the other side and around the cabin a number of Federal soldiers were killed. These were picked up after the battle and buried under a tall pecan tree about a quarter of a mile from the cabin and south of it. They were subsequently removed, when the Federal dead were collected into the various national burying grounds. The spot, however, where they were first buried upon the

Legree plantation is clearly and plainly marked by a tall pecan tree, that still stands with a sentinel-like appearance, as though it was keeping watch over the spot. There was, however, one of the Federal dead left upon the place. He was wounded in the battle and left in a cotton-gin, where he afterward died, and was buried by citizens under a large and ancient fig tree, about one hundred yards from the residence of Simon Legree, where his remains still repose. As I stood by his grave I could not help but think that possibly, in his early youth, he had seen the play of "Uncle Tom's Cabin" rendered upon the theaters of the North; and possibly been induced thereby to rush quickly into the action when the welkin of war rang. If this was so with himself or the others who died there around that cabin, is it not a strange meditation for us to muse upon now, that he should subsequently die in the very shadow of the cabin, where his dying groans would echo and re-echo as they faded away, from wall to wall of that historic house, that in the dreams of his youth he had often visited? And what may seem stranger still, the fact that he was laid to rest at last beneath the shadows of a fig tree, that was most likely planted by the hand of Simon Legree.

Just then there came a puff of wind from the south, and in passing the grave of Simon Legree it rattled the dry fallen forest leaves around and over it, and passing onward next dolefully mourned through the open doors and paneless windows of his moss-covered residence. Thence it swept along over the soldiers' lonely grave, where it seemed to rearrange the dry and falling grasses of that little mound.

Amid this historic scene and commotion of autumn winds and leaves, we could not help thinking of the rapid mutations of time, and thought we could see all these leveled in the dust of the future. But we could not see to where mention of them would be obliterated from history's pages.

The cabin is now on exhibition in the enclosure of the Libby Prison War Museum on Wabash avenue, Chicago, Ill. In visiting the city don't fail to come and see this world-renowned house, and when there, by no means fail to purchase a souvenir for the dear ones at home. We have a great variety of walking sticks, beautiful ratan, that grew upon the plantation, and cotton balls from the plantation, done up in nice boxes with a clear cut picture of the cabin on the box. Also a number of finely executed photographs, taken en the place, showing everything from the residence of Legree to his grave. A full set of these would be so instructive to one's family that you cannot afford to return home without them. They are made both ways, so you can take stereoscopic or cabinet views.

There will also be on exhibition in the cabin, a fine picture of Simon Legree. This has been kept by a lady living in the parish ever since before his death.

P. S.—Since writing the above, I have received the following letter from Rev. Charles Beecher. He is that brother referred to by Mrs. Stowe as being in New Orleans at the time, and from whom she derived the information concerning the character of Legree. The letter was written to me in response to one I had written him shortly before. In order to assist you in understanding what we were writing about, let me say that Natchitoches is fifty-two miles above Alexandria, on Red river. The Legree plantation is thirty miles above Alexandria and all on the west side or same side of the river. This puts the plantation just thirty miles

above Alexandria and twenty-two miles below Natchitoches. Further, I would ask you to compare this letter of his with what she says of him in that chapter of
her book entitled, "Concluding Remarks." Do this
and you will catch the full import and meaning of his
letter.

"WYSOX, PA., Nov. 29, 1892.

" Mr. D. B. CORLEY.

" *Dear Sir:*

"It must have been some time in 1837 or '8, that I
visited Alexandria and Natchitoches. I remember incidents, but not names or dates. I cannot remember
where the plantation was, nor the name of its owner,
which gave my sister a hint for the character of Legree.
I have no records of any kind of that Red river trip,
and do not recognize the name you mention.

" Respectfully,

"CHARLES BEECHER."

TESTIMONIALS.

State of Louisiana, }
Parish of Natchitoches. }

My name is L. Chopin. I am forty-two years old
and was born and raised in Natchitoches Parish,
Louisiana. In the year 1852 my father bought at public sale the Robert McAlpin plantation, situated on
Red river in the southern portion of the parish, and
moved upon the place shortly afterward. The occasion of the plantation being sold was on account of
McAlpin's death. He being a bachelor the estate was
wound up and the proceeds distributed among distant
relatives.

Outside of a few years spent in Europe at school, I
have lived on the plantation all my life, and until the

Texas and Pacific railroad run through the place I lived in the old McAlpin residence. A portion of the old residence was torn down by the railroad, and the roadbed now runs through it, the balance of the building being used as a section house.

When my father first moved on the place, or at least a few years afterward, he had one of the two rows of China trees in front of the house cut down because it obstructed the view and made too much of shade. I still remember, although a child at the time, the great time we children had helping the negroes pull on the ropes which were fastened to the tops of the trees being cut down to prevent them from falling over and damaging those that were to be kept.

After the war my father commenced tearing down the cabins from the negro quarters and scattering them over the plantation, as the negroes objected to living in the old "quarters." It "looked too much like slavery," so they said.

After I assumed the control of the place at my father's death, I continued tearing down and moving the cabins, and there is now standing on the grounds where the negro quarters were located only the cabin known as Uncle Tom's cabin. This I never moved, and have religiously kept ever since on account of the tradition connected with it, which makes it the cabin that "Uncle Tom" occupied on the Legree plantation.

Tradition has it that McAlpin was the Legree of Mrs. Stowe's book. From all reports of white and black he was a very cruel master to his slaves, and when drunk would abuse them dreadfully and is said to have caused the death of several of them. He was a very hard drinker and died from the effects of drink. He was buried on a little hill near the residence, and his grave can still be seen there, although very much dilapidated. His is the only white man's grave there; the place has always and is still used as a plantation burial ground, and quite a number of negroes are buried around his grave.

When quite young I knew the place as the Legree plantation and the cabin as Uncle Tom's, and it is well known as "Uncle Tom's" cabin and believed to be so, not only here, but all over the country, as I have at several times received letters from the different states asking for pieces of boards from the cabin to be kept as relics.

For years I have kept the cabin just for the sake of its association with Mrs. Stowe's book, without any thought of its ever being of any money value and without a thought of its ever being moved from the plantation, but lately I have been approached by parties from Chicago and New York who have offered to buy the cabin with the view of bringing it to the World's Fair at Chicago. Those offers I refused, and refused at first to entertain any idea of its being moved from the place even temporarily, but have finally consented to its being moved to Chicago for the World's Fair, after repeated representations were made me that such a cabin, so closely connected with such a well-known book as Uncle Tom's Cabin, was in a manner public property and the opportunity should be given to everybody to see it.

L. CHOPIN.

Sworn to and subscribed before me this 15th Oct., 1892.

[SEAL.]   JNO. A. BARLOW,
                          D. Clk. 10th D. C.

STATEMENT OF MRS. VALERY GAIENNIE.

I knew Mr. Robert McAlpin very well. I used to

live on the Gaiennie plantation, about two miles from the McAlpin plantation. I often visited Mr. McAlpin at his house; he was very amiable to us, but I have always heard that he was very mean to his slaves. When I was young there was a lady from the North that visited Mr. McAlpin. She did not associate with us; did not care to know us it seemed, and being a Yankee we did not care to have anything to do with her either. I have heard that the lady was the one that wrote "Uncle Tom's Cabin," but I don't know for certain that she is. My husband told me that the Uncle Tom of the "book" was the old Uncle Tom that used to work for McAlpin. I remember Uncle Tom very well. He used to cross me over the river when we used to go to McAlpin, and used to wait around the yard and table; he was a respectful and kind old man. I have always heard that Mr. McAlpin was very mean to him, but I do not know this of my own knowledge. I only heard my slaves say that Mr. McAlpin used to whip Uncle Tom and treat him very harshly. Uncle Tom always looked very sad, and I used to feel very sorry for him; the fact that we heard of Mr. McAlpin's cruelty to him made us pity him. I have always heard that most of McAlpin's cruelty was done when he was under the influence of liquor, and he had the reputation of being a great drunkard, but before ladies he was gentlemanly. I never saw any cruel act to his slaves.

MRS. VALERY GAIENNIE.

Sworn to and subscribed before me this Nov. 26th, '92.

[SEAL.]   H. M. HYAMS,
                            Clk. 10th D. C., La.

STATEMENT OF JOHN SYLVESTRE.

My name is John Sylvestre. I am eighty-seven years

old and I used to live at Monette's Ferry, two miles from McAlpin. I used to pick cotton for Mr. McAlpin; he was very cruel to his slaves, and when he was drunk he did not care what he did to his slaves, and used to beat them. Old Uncle Tom used to work about the yard and McAlpin was very cruel to him.

JOHN SYLVESTRE.

Sworn to and subscribed before me this 26th day of November, 1892.

[SEAL.]   H. M. HYAMS,
                          Clk. 10th D. C., La.

STATE OF LOUISIANA, }
Parish of Natchitoches. }

Before me, the undersigned authority, duly qualified, personally came and appeared Samuel Parson, who being by me sworn according to law, and who is also known to me as a reliable and truthful person and who deposes as follows:

I am 78 years of age. I knew Robert McAlpin well. He lived on and owned the plantation which L. Chopin now owns, on Cane river in the parish. I have lived 57 years in this parish. I worked for some time on a place near McAlpin's. His neighbors all knew him as a man who was excessively cruel to his slaves. I remember whilst at work, and when he would pass, the men would all curse him as he passed on account of his cruelty to his slaves. It was commonly circulated and believed in the neighborhood that several of his slaves had died from abusive treatment received from him. The place I worked at was two miles from McAlpin's. It was generally known and believed in the neighborhood that Mrs. Stowe wrote her work "Uncle Tom's Cabin" whilst on a visit to McAlpin, and that McAlpin owned a slave Tom.

I know there is a cabin on the place now owned by Chopin which has always been pointed out to me and has always been known as the cabin of Uncle Tom.

I am getting old and my memory is not very good. I could relate different acts of cruelty by him to his slaves, but it has been so long I can't now recall them. I know he was a very cruel and severe master. McAlpin is buried on the Chopin place.

S. PARSON.

Sworn to and subscribed before me at Natchitoches, La., this 28th November, 1892.

[SEAL.]
JNO. A. BARLOW,
Deputy Clerk.

NATCHITOCHES, LA., Oct. 15, 1892.

I, the undersigned, deputy clerk of the 10th Dist. Court Parish of Natchitoches, La., do hereby certify that I am well acquainted with Lanny Chopin and Phanor Breazeale, having known them for 15 or 20 years past; that they are both credible and reliable gentlemen, and any statement made by them is worthy of all confidence.

I further certify that both of the gentlemen named reside in this parish. P. P. Breazeale being now the district attorney for this, the 10th Judicial District of the State of Louisiana, and Mr. Chopin being a planter and manager and owner in the proportion of about one-half of the Givanovich-Chopin Oil Co. of this city.

Witness my hand and official seal, Oct. 15, 1892.

[SEAL.]
JNO. A. BARLOW,
Deputy Clerk.

NATCHITOCHES, LA., Oct. 15, 1892.

I certify that there is situated on the plantation on Red river, in this parish, a cabin—which is notoriously recognized as "Uncle Tom's Cabin." The plantation is now owned by L. Chopin, and was formerly the Mc-Alpin plantation; and passersby on the trains of the T. & P. R. R. Co. almost invariably (when cognizant of the facts) request that Chopin's plantation and the cabin be shown them.

It is traditional that McAlpin was a hard master on his slaves, and that his cruelty caused the death of several of them.

[SEAL.]   JNO. A. BARLOW,
                                          D. Clk. 10th D. C.

STATE OF LOUISIANA,   }
Parish of Natchitoches. }

Before me, the undersigned authority duly qualified, personally came and appeared Richard McLean, to me well known as a truthful and reliable person, who being by me duly sworn, according to law, deposes and says:

That he is 83 years of age, and has resided in the parish of Natchitoches for the past 58 years.

I knew Robert McAlpin who formerly lived in this parish, on the plantation now owned by L. Chopin.

I knew from general reputation that McAlpin was a very severe master and hard on his slaves. And I have always heard that "Uncle Tom's Cabin" was situated on the McAlpin plantation, and that the book of Mrs. Stowe was written whilst on a visit to McAlpin— which book was called *Uncle Tom's Cabin*, by her.

                                     RICHARD MCLEAN.

Sworn to and subscribed before me this 28th day of November, 1892.

[SEAL.]   JNO. A. BARLOW,
                                          D. Clk. D. C.

NEW ORLEANS, LA., November 18, 1891.

I hereby certify that the following statement is correct, basing my opinion on the statements, history and traditions of old settlers and people living there, that the *original Uncle Tom's Cabin* is situated at the station of Chopin, near Cane river, a part of Red river parish of Natchitoches, State of Louisiana, on Texas and Pacific railroad.

I was president of Chopin Lumber Company at that place, and the logs sawed at our mills were cut from the land formerly owned by McAlpin, and the said McAlpin was the Legree of the book; and from all I could learn he fully justified the authoress, Harriet Beecher Stowe, in using him under a disguised name to illustrate such character as was desired to show heartlessness and cruelty. McAlpin was the original Legree, and this cabin was Uncle Tom's. The present owner of the property I have known for years (L. Chopin), and he is an honorable gentleman, and his statements can be relied upon.

Yours truly,
C. S. BURT.

Sworn to and subscribed before a qualified notary public in and for the Parish of Orleans, State of Louisiana, by Charles S. Burt, on this 18th day of November, A. D. 1891, as witness my hand and seal.

JNO. I. WARD,

[SEAL.]   Notary Public.

NEW ORLEANS, LA., Nov. 18, 1891.

To WHOM IT MAY CONCERN:

Having been a resident of Chopin, La., for a number of years, I would say that I have always heard the *log cabin*, situated about four hundred yards from the Texas and Pacific railroad, spoken of by the old residents as the original of Uncle Tom's Cabin, and that Mr. McAlpin, who formerly owned the Chopin plantation, was known as a person fully capable of being the Legree of the romance of Mrs. Stowe. I am fully convinced, from information I gained there, that the above statement is correct.

WM. P. LUCK,
Traveling Salesman for C. S. Burt.

Sworn to and subscribed before me by William P. Luck, at New Orleans, La., on the 18th day of November, A. D. 1891, as witness my hand and seal as a duly-qualified notary public in and for the Parish of Orleans, State of Louisiana, aforesaid.

JNO. I. WARD,
[SEAL.] Notary Public.

I hereby certify, that having lived a number of months at Chopin, Louisiana, I had always heard a certain old log cabin situated a few hundred yards from the railroad track referred to as "Uncle Tom's Cabin," and it was admitted by people living thereabout without question, that the cabin was the one formerly occupied by Harriet Beecher Stowe's famous "Uncle Tom." It is also a fact that the former owner of the plantation upon which this cabin stood was an exceedingly cruel man to his slaves, and it was from him that Mrs. Stowe undoubtedly took her character of "Legree." His grave is not far from the old plantation house.

ARTHUR M. ODELL.

Sworn to and subscribed before me this 14th day of December, 1891, at New Orleans, La.

[SEAL.] J. ZACH. SPEARING,
Notary Public.

THE STATE OF LOUISIANA, }
City of New Orleans. }

My name is T. G. Thurston, and I now live in the city of New Orleans. I was born at Saline in Texas in 1844. My father moved to the city of New Orleans in 1846, at which place I have resided ever since. My father's mother was the daughter of Gen. Gates of revolutionary fame. Hence I am the great grandson of the general.

I have always had and still have a due regard for the truth in all matters. In 1852 I went on a side-wheel steamboat from New Orleans to Shreveport, La. Though quite young, I remember the trip well, for it was my father's boat, and further it was the first side-wheel boat that ever went up Red river. It was on this trip up the river in 1852 that I heard for the first time of Uncle Tom's cabin, and I heard then that it was situated on Red river in Louisiana. But I do not remember to have seen the cabin then.

I grew up to manhood and entered the Confederate army in the late war, where I served respectively under Gens. Beauregard, Bragg, Johnson and Hood, as courier to each. And when the war was over returned home to New Orleans.

I am at present acting as conductor of a Pullman sleeping car on the T. & P. R. R., which road passes between the cabin of Uncle Tom and the residence of Robt. McAlpin, alias Simon Legree, in the lower portion of Natchitoches Parish, La. I have been running the road about seven years and have shown to many people this cabin as Uncle Tom's cabin. The old people along in that immediate section say it is the cabin, and I verily believe it to be the cabin. Of course I cannot say that I know it to be so, but I can say and do swear that from the best information upon the subject that there is no doubt in my mind that it is Uncle Tom's cabin, and I do so swear.

T. G. THURSTON.

Subscribed and sworn to before me, a duly qualified notary public, in and for the Parish of Orleans, State of Louisiana, this 22d day of October, 1892.

[SEAL.]   J. D. TAYLOR,
Notary Public.

What Hon. R. T. Vinson, mayor of Shreveport, Louisiana, says in a recent letter:

DECEMBER 7, 1892.

Capt. Chopin, Natchitoches, La.:

DEAR CAPTAIN: It affords me pleasure to testify in reference to Uncle Tom's cabin. I have known of this cabin for years, and believe it to be the original. I tried to purchase it from you to be sent on to the exposition. I also interviewed the old citizens of your neighborhood, and all agree that the cabin was occupied by Uncle Tom during the time he was owned by McAlpin. This is certainly the cabin that Mrs. Stowe wrote about.   Respectfully,

R. T. VINSON, Mayor.

STATE OF LOUISIANA,   }
Parish of Natchitoches. }

Before me, the undersigned authority duly qualified, personally came and appeared Wellington Slidell, a resident of the parish and state above named, and to me well known, who being by me first duly sworn according to law, deposes and says, as follows:

"My name is Wellington Slidell. I am a colored man and am about eighty years of age. I knew Mr. Robert McAlpin and remember him well. He bought me in New Orleans when I was eight years old, and I was owned by him as a slave up to the time of his death, at which time I was thirty-four years old. McAlpin died on what is now called the Chopin plantation and is buried on that place.

"McAlpin, when drinking, was mean and very cruel to his slaves. On one occasion I remember we were working in some new ground, which had just been put in cultivation. It was so cold at the time we had to work with our coats on. The cook, whose name was Mary, didn't cook dinner to suit him and he whipped her unmercifully and tied her, entirely naked, to a stake. He broke her jaw with his walking stick. When he finished whipping her she could not walk, and we had to carry her into the kitchen. She died that night about nine o'clock.

"Mr. McAlpin was very mean to Tom and another slave he owned named William.

"He was harder on his house servants and yard boys, and meaner to them than the balance of us, because they were around him more when he was drunk.

"McAlpin had two yellow girls (mulattoes) that worked in the house. Their names were Rebecca and Lucinda. He did not allow any of us field hands to talk to these girls—he kept them as his wives.

"On one occasion my brother talked with one of these girls, and he whipped him nearly to death. He sold Rebecca and kept Lucinda because she would not let us talk to her. He sent Rebecca to New Orleans and sold her after keeping her several years, because he was afraid she might poison him on account of his cruelty to her, as when he was sick she gave him his medicine.

"I am so old and infirm and my memory has failed me, so I can't recall much that happened whilst I was owned by McAlpin, but I do know we (his slaves) were all mighty glad when he died."

his
WELLINGTON + SLIDELL.
mark
declaring he could not write.

Sworn to and subscribed before me at Natchitoches, La., this 8th day of December, 1892.

[SEAL.]   JNO. A. BARLOW,
                               Dy. Clk. D. C.

NOTE.—The Lucinda mentioned in the above statement is none other than the Cassey of Mrs. Stowe's book. She is still remembered by many of the old plantation negroes of that neighborhood as the finest formed negress they ever looked upon.

The *Democrat Review*, of Natchitoches, La., of Dec. 2, 1892, says:

UNCLE TOM'S CABIN.—REALITY OF THE WORLD-
RENOWNED FICTION.

The countless thousands who have wept over the pages of Mrs. Harriet Beecher Stowe's realistic recital of "Uncle Tom's" thraldom, will certainly embrace the opportunity to visit the cabin in which "Uncle Tom" lived and died. That opportunity will be given to all, for the cabin will be exhibited at the World's Columbian Exposition. The cabin is without doubt the genuine little hut that sheltered Uncle Tom. Tradition, and the corroborative testimony of many old citizens of this parish, are guarantees of its authenticity.

Recently accounts have been published in several journals, notably in the "Home and Farm," of Louisville, Ky., under date of November 15, 1892, from the pen of Bill Arp, and in the Chicago "Tribune," of November 21, 1892, this latter being accompanied with truthful pictures of "Uncle Tom's Cabin," "Church on the Plantation," and the "Robert McAlpin Home."

These buildings still exist. The plantation on which they stand is on the Texas & Pacific railroad, on Cane river, twenty-seven miles below Natchitoches, in this parish. The railroad cuts off a part of the home of McAlpin.

Mrs. Stowe, in her work, describes Legree's home as a low two-story structure, surrounded by wide verandas supported by brick pillars, with two rows of China trees in front of the house. This is an exact description of the McAlpin house, except that the back galleries have since been closed in, and made into rooms—the floors of these improvised rooms still retaining the usual inclination given to a gallery; and with the further exception that one row of trees was cut down by Mr. Chopin's father.

McAlpin owned a slave by the name of "Uncle Tom," and reliable witnesses now testify that his treatment of this slave was particularly harsh.

Robert McAlpin was a Northerner of Scotch descent, who in his sober moments was genial and hospitable. But he was greatly intemperate, when he became cruel, brutal and harsh to his slaves, a fit subject from whom to draw such a character as Legree.

And we have no doubt, that Mrs. Stowe's brother, who visited this section of Red river, as she herself says in her admirable book, referred to McAlpin when he related to her his experiences with a Red river planter whom he had found so cruel, and that McAlpin was the original Legree of the work.

The cabin in which the negro, "Uncle Tom," owned by McAlpin, lived, is in a fair state of preservation. The logs and shingles of which it is constructed are of cypress, a timber that withstands the decaying touch of time.

These landmarks of the great novel coincide so closely with Mrs. Stowe's descriptions that they have been accepted as the originals on which her imagination built her remarkable and thrilling history.

By those living on the place and in the parish, it

has long been known as "Uncle Tom's Cabin," and the plantation as that of "Legree." The place was purchased by Mr. J. B. Chopin, the father of the present owner, in 1852, at the death of Robert McAlpin.

For a number of years Mr. L. Chopin has had it guarded by a faithful colored servitor, to prevent its being razed to the ground by eager relic hunters. In truth, a number of board slabs nailed on the logs were carried off by curious visitors who had learned its history.

Some months ago this writer, then a resident of Shreveport, was aware of an attempt of prominent citizens to purchase outright this same structure, to transplant it entire to the World's Fair, as a relic, around which clustered a world-wide fame, given it by fiction. Mr. Chopin then, as he has repeatedly since, declined to part with the building.

Several weeks ago Mr. D. B. Corley visited this city in company with G. E. Ward, of Abilene, Tex., and took a number of photographic views in and around this city, and among others in the parish, the famed mementoes of Uncle Tom.

When this article meets the gaze of the readers, Uncle Tom's cabin will have left its birthplace and long years of rest on the soil where it was originally built, and have been transplanted to Chicago. It has not been sold to Mr. Corley, but only leased to him by the present owner. It is to be returned in its entirety when the lease expires.

Tradition, the belief among old residents, black and white, the coincidence of the reality in substantiation of the description, confirms the general belief that this cabin is the true Uncle Tom's cabin of Mrs. Stowe's novel.

Natchitoches, settled in 1710, is replete with ancient landmarks, of a century dropped into the irrevocable past, but "Uncle Tom's cabin" is a mile-stone on the highway of life that has its "confirmations strong as proofs of holy writ."

The *Enterprise*, of Natchitoches, La., of Dec. 1, 1892, says:

The famous novel which bears the strange title of "Uncle Tom's Cabin," which was given to the world during the excitement over the fugitive slave law, and which had much to do with bringing about the terrible four years' conflict between the North and the South, is still a book that attracts the greatest interest throughout the civilized world, and everything connected with it is sought for with the keenest interest. So when the announcement is made that the home of Uncle Tom is to be placed on exhibition at the World's Fair, the truly interested and the skeptic asks, "Is it really Uncle Tom's cabin or a fake?"

There is no written evidence, or notarial act to prove that this little log hut which is being taken to Chicago was the home of Mrs. Stowe's Uncle Tom, nor is there any to prove it is not, *but there is* tradition well authenticated to substantiate the claim that this was Uncle Tom's cabin and that the old McAlpin plantation situated on the Texas and Pacific railroad in the lower portion of this parish, and now owned by L. Chopin, having been bought by Mr. Chopin's father in 1852 from the McAlpin succession, is where were enacted the scenes described in Mrs. Stowe's famous story.

Why is this believed to be Uncle Tom's cabin? Because every scene about the old McAlpin plantation fits Mrs. Stowe's description to a nicety. The cabin, the residence and location *all* tally with the picture drawn in "Uncle Tom's Cabin;" and tradition tells us that Robert McAlpin was such a character as Mrs. Stowe's Simon Legree; and her own evidence given in one of the reviews of her work wherein she states that the character called Simon Legree was suggested by a letter from her brother then in New Orleans, who had visited a planter on the Red river; and the further evidence, which is obtainable from old residents, that her brother visited Mr. McAlpin, is proof positive so far as circumstantial evidence can make it that Mr. McAlpin was the real Simon Legree, and it is not unreasonable to believe that Mrs. Stowe's Uncle Tom is the same Uncle Tom who is known to have lived upon the same plantation.

The Chicago *Tribune* of Sunday, November 20, published a lengthy article upon the subject with pictures of Uncle Tom's cabin, Robert McAlpin's home and the old plantation colored Methodist church.

The cut in the *Tribune* presents true pictures of these buildings. The one of the cabin is perfect.

So well satisfied are all who have taken trouble to investigate, that the cabin, claimed to have been the home of this now noted character, is the one and only one entitled to bear the name given to Mrs. Stowe's book. Numberless offers to buy from Mr. Chopin this property outright have been made within the past several years, but which have been steadily refused, because Mr. Chopin feels confident he has in his possession the real "Uncle Tom's Cabin," and does not care to part with it at any price.

But last week Mr. Chopin closed a bargain with Judge D. B. Corley of Abilene, Texas, for a five years' lease of the cabin, with good and solvent security for its return and re-erection upon the same spot where it now stands, upon the expiration of the lease.

Judge Corley begins removing the cabin to-day; and by the first of next year it will be on exhibition in Chicago.

Many of the strips which closed the cracks between the logs have been torn away by relic seekers. Only a year or two ago Jay Gould, in company with his daughter, stopped upon his tour of inspection of his Texas Pacific R. R. line, to visit this now historic cabin, and carried away with him a shingle from its roof as a memento. For the past several years Mr. Chopin has been forced to keep a watch over this building to protect it from the ravenous relic seekers.

The New Orleans *Times-Democrat* of December 4, 1892, says:

Half asleep, scarcely half dressed and with the remainder of my clothes in my hand, I tumbled hurriedly off the west-bound Texas and Pacific train three-quarters of an hour before daylight yesterday morning. I was ticketed for Chopin, La., and the sleeping-car conductor had solemnly promised to have me called forty-five minutes before the train could reach here. Foolishly relying upon his promise I slept "like a log" until the negro porter called me not ten minutes before arrival at my destination. The morning was warm and murky, without even the faintest gleam of starlight to relieve the thick darkness after the train with its subdued lights from half-darkened windows had swept off up the road and faded from view. Standing between two bales of cotton on the station platform, I completed the task of dressing (barely commenced on the train) and then waited for the coming of daylight.

I had come here for the purpose of looking over the

premises, which were in Mrs. Stowe's mind as a model when she penned the tragic scenes with which her widely known novel, "Uncle Tom's Cabin," is brought to a climax and almost to a close.

Mr. D. B. Corley, ex-mayor of Abilene, Tex., had obtained the right of exhibiting what is supposed to have been "Uncle Tom's Cabin" at the World's Fair, and upon his invitation I had come to Chopin to look over what is here believed to have been the model after which Mrs. Stowe designed her Legree plantation, and to hear what I could of the former owner of the property.

Of course, in the light of an intimate acquaintance with the authentic history and traditions of slavery in Louisiana, any sane person cannot but realize that the pictures of unbridled license and brutal tyranny associated with Simon Legree's plantation have been greatly overdrawn; but quite aside from this, it is well known that this same story was a powerfully written one, and that it was, without doubt, one of the most aggressive agents in the making of subsequent history that has found a place in American fiction.

For this reason, therefore, no matter to what extent one may discredit the tone and methods of Harriet Beecher Stowe's masterpiece, whatever may be found remaining in tangible form of the models used by her in the designing of her fiction, must be looked upon as historic relics of no ordinary value.

WHAT IS CLAIMED BY MR. CORLEY.

The claim made by Mr. Corley is substantially as follows:

"What is now the Chopin plantation is the model from which Mrs. Stowe sketched the Legree plantation, that the former owner of this property, Robert McAlpin, was the Simon Legree of the novel; that a small cabin, 16x18, which still stands upon its original site in the old quarters, is the cabin in which Uncle Tom spent the last sad months of his servitude; that the greater part of the Legree mansion still stands upon the spot where Uncle Tom first saw it, and in short, that in just so far as this portion of the novel are founded on fact, so far are these historic relics genuine.

"Possibly the best way to weigh the claims made by Mr. Corley will be to compare the descriptions in the novel with the models after which it is claimed they were drawn.

"The novel describes Simon Legree as 'a short, broad, muscular man, in a checked shirt considerably open at the bosom, and pantaloons much the worse for dirt and wear. * * * He was evidently, though short, of gigantic strength. His round, bullet head, large, light gray eyes, with their shaggy, sandy eyebrows and stiff, wiry, sun-burned hair, were rather unprepossessing items, it is to be confessed; his large, coarse mouth was distended with tobacco, the juice of which, from time to time, he ejected from him with great decision and explosive force; his hands were immensely large, hairy, sun-burned, freckled and very dirty, and garnished with long nails in a very foul condition.'"

The story also pictures Legree as a hard drinker, violent in temper, cruel, superstitious and licentious. He never employed an overseer, but only two negro drivers. He is described as a planter on Red river, but at the same time the story tells that on the journey to the plantation, Uncle Tom and other slaves purchased at the same time were "trailing wearily behind a rude wagon over a ruder road. * * * It was a wild, forsaken road, now winding through dreary pine barrens, where the wind whispered mournfully, and now over log causeways, through long cypress swamps, the doleful trees rising out of the slimy, spongy ground, hung with long wreaths of funereal black moss."

Legree is also described as having been born in New England.

THE PROTOTYPE OF LEGREE.

The supposed prototype of Legree was a man named Robert McAlpin. Senator Henry, who in his early boyhood was employed in the store of his uncle, who was then doing business in Natchitoches long before the war, remembers Robert McAlpin very well, though he had seen little or nothing of him except when he was visiting Natchitoches for business or pleasure. He was a man of light complexion with reddish or sandy hair and beard. Though considerably below medium height he was very broad and heavily built, weighing between 180 and 200 pounds. He was nearly always half drunk or more on the occasion of these visits, and was very much liked by the men and boys of the town for his good-natured and jovial, rollicking disposition. He was disposed to spend his money freely, and was very fond of entertaining friends or acquaintances at his plantation, which was always very liberally stocked with good wines and liquors. Mr. Henry did not remember to have heard any stories about his extraordinary cruelty to his slaves, though as thirty miles of bad road lay between Natchitoches and McAlpin's plantation he admits that he might have been severe with his slaves without any intimation of

it reaching Natchitoches in those days of slow loco-
motion over bad roads. He had since heard stories of
McAlpin's extraordinary cruelty to his slaves, but he
had always been of opinion that they had been exaggerated.

Mrs. Valery Gaiennie, who lived on the Gaiennie
plantation, being within visiting distance of the McAlpin plantation, remembers Robert McAlpin well. She
had often visited his place. He was always very cour-
teous and gentlemanly in the presence of ladies, but
his extraordinary cruelties to his slaves were very commonly talked about by both whites and blacks on the
neighboring plantations. It was very generally believed
that these excesses were the result of drunkenness, but
as he was a very hard and almost constant drinker, his
slaves led a hard life. Mrs. Gaiennie also remembers
an elderly negro on the place who used to be called
"Uncle Tom." She describes him as a well-behaved,
respectable and kind-hearted old man, but he always
used to wear a serious, sad look, which caused her and
other lady visitors to the McAlpin plantation to feel
sorry for him. It was also reported in those days that
McAlpin was particularly mean and cruel to "Uncle
Tom," who was sadder, more serious and much better
bred than a vast majority of Red river slaves. He
used to ferry visitors across the river, look after the
yard, and wait upon the table. It was generally supposed that McAlpin's cruelty to "Uncle Tom" was the
chief cause of the slave's subdued and dejected manner.

Other ladies of the Cane river settlements corrobo-
rate these statements, and no better evidence of Mc-
Alpin's extraordinary cruelty can be had than the fact
that from the time of his death up to within a comparatively recent date, the negroes and the more supersti-

tious of the whites have believed that the place was
haunted by his ghost, which has been one of the terrors
of that whole region. One of the stories still believed
about Robert McAlpin is that having once become
very angry with a slave, he sewed him up in a sack
and drowned him in Cane river. McAlpin never en-
trusted his business to an overseer, but employed negro
drivers only.

Another circumstance that may be mentioned in
this connection which, while it fails to show any connection between McAlpin and "Legree," is in itself
rather amusing. One of the ladies who knew McAlpin
intimately as a neighbor, says that at one time he had a
lady from the North visiting him. She says that this
lady was not disposed to associate with the ladies of
the neighborhood and, "as she was a Yankee, we did
not care to cultivate her acquaintance." The narrator
adds that after the novel came out they were of the
opinion that this mysterious visitor was its author.

IDENTITY OF THE LOCATION.

As to the identity of the location of the McAlpin
plantation with that of the "Legree" place, it will be
remembered that while the former was on Cane river
the latter was said to be on Red river. Long ago, and
not very long before Legree's time, what has since been
known as Cane river was the main channel of Red
river, and that until railway transportation began to
cut away the Red river steamboat trade, all the country supposed to be tributary to the Red river trade was
embraced in the general term "Red river country."
Besides this it will be remembered that the novel
describes a long and weary journey from the steamboat landing. The McAlpin place is about ten miles

from an old landing on Red river, and the old trail
between these points was very like that described in
the novel.

The description of the "Legree" mansion corresponds very accurately with what the McAlpin residence used to be when Mr. Chopin's father purchased it
early in the "fifties." The story says:

The wagon rolled up a weedy gravel walk under a
noble avenue of China trees, whose graceful forms and
ever springing foliage seemed to be the only things
there that neglect could not daunt or alter—like noble
spirits so deeply rooted in goodness as to flourish and
grow stronger amid discouragement and decay.

The house had been large and handsome. It was
built in a manner common to the South, a wide veranda
of two stories running around every part of the house,
into which every outer door opened, the lower tier
being supported by brick pillars.

As the McAlpin mansion stands upon a point
made by the junction of a deep gulch or bayou with
Cane river, the caving of the banks of both streams
(common to all streams in the Red river country) has
had the effect of somewhat reducing what were some
time spacious grounds surrounding it. The present
owner of the property, Mr. Chopin, well remembers
when the outer row of China trees forming the avenue
described were cut down by the order of his father,
who purchased the plantation shortly after McAlpin's
death. These trees were cut down because the caving of
the bank of Cane river had caused them to sink down
several feet below the level of the inner row, which
still stands flourishing in front of the house.

The veranda at the front of what remains of the
house still stands just as Mrs. Stowe has described it, but

at the back of the house it has been inclosed with rough woodwork (not at all in keeping with the original building) for the purpose of adding to the capacity of the house. At the north end the veranda was long ago cut away, and the south end of the building encroaching upon the line of the Texas and Pacific railway was cut away to the extent of some twenty-two feet to make room for the roadbed.

The interior, as well as the exterior of this house, corresponds well with the general description in the book. Before the cutting away of the south end to make room for the railway, the house was 75 feet long, but without the broad galleries could not have been more than about 20 feet wide. It has an old-fashioned, high pitched roof, whose eaves extend to form the veranda roof. The roof is covered with shingles, thickly crusted with dark green moss. They are of split cypress, longer and much heavier than the shingles of to-day. Though the house wears the look of extreme old age, it is evident that it was a very highly finished and handsome residence in its time. The joists supporting the upper floors are not only smoothly planed, but delicately beaded. All the original casements are richly ornamented with beaded edges and deep moldings, while the doors are of six panels, elaborately bordered with fine moldings. Beneath the eaves and in certain portions less exposed to climatic influences, the walls show traces of having been painted white, while there are distinct traces of green on the old broken shutters; but the general effect of the whole exterior is that dark, steely gray, indicative of three-quarters of a century or more of weather stain.

The old house stands facing the convex of a sharp

bend in Cane river, which only a few hundred yards
southeastward cuts off rather abruptly a wooded spur
that juts out of the hill country extending away westward to the Texas line. Almost parallel with the
course of Cane river at this point the railway cuts
through this same spur. Its course is through a natural
depression which long ago marked the site of an old
wagon trail from Red river, the railway cutting being
about fifty feet deep. Sheltered by this same wooded
spur is a broad stretch of bottom lands extending
away to the southwest, ending in a swamp which in
turn gives place to a small chain of shallow, marshy
lakes, whose outlet is a small bayou. This, as it
approaches its junction with the Cane river, runs within
a few yards of the back door of the old McAlpin residence and is well sheltered by comparatively high and
precipitous banks. On the stretch of bottoms between
the spur and this bayou already described, is a great
field of cotton land which is somewhat wedge-shaped,
with the apex reaching up to the McAlpin mansion.
Some two or three hundred yards from the old house,
extending in the direction of the swamps, is the site of
the old "quarters" of the plantation, but just now only
one of these cabins remains.

UNCLE TOM'S CABIN.

Since Mr. Chopin, the present owner of the property,
succeeded to it, the negroes complained about "living
in a bunch" in the old-fashioned way, and in compli-
ance with their wishes the cabins were scattered about
the place; Mr. Chopin leaving only one upon its
original site, and this was left because it had always
been known as "Uncle Tom's Cabin" since before the
property passed into the hands of the Chopin family

in 1852. In former times it had a low, broad gallery, or awning, extending along the front, but this tumbled down some years ago, and within a comparatively short time Mr. Chopin has built a similar one on the opposite side of the cabin. The old cabin has a steeply pitched roof of thick, long cypress shingles, thickly encrusted with dark green moss. It is built of cypress logs, which seem to have been from twelve to eighteen inches in diameter, but either sawed or hewn flat on both sides to a thickness of not more than six or seven inches. The joints made by the logs at the corners of the building have been closely finished, in dovetail fashion, and not merely "saddled," as most of the old backwoods' frontier cabins used to be. It originally had merely a ground floor, and the gallery was also without any artificial flooring. There is a large opening for a fireplace, but the big brick chimney which formerly stood against the house and extended above the gable has crumbled into ruins. Mr. Chopin knew this as "Uncle Tom's Cabin" from his earliest childhood, and it was known by that name when his father bought the plantation and before any one in the neighborhood had learned of the existence of Mrs. Stowe's novel.

It may be mentioned here that it has been customary to point out the kitchen of the old mansion as Uncle Tom's cabin to save the real cabin from being despoiled by relic hunters.

The position of the McAlpin mansion, the site of the old quarters, and the peculiar course of the swamps and the bayous all accurately fit the leading events described in such minute detail in her tragic story of the Legree plantation.

THE FLIGHT OF CASSEY AND EMELINE.

Cassey and Emeline are said to have left the house on their pretended flight, and passing down by the quarters fled to the swamp beyond, when Legree called after them. Such is the peculiar topography of the McAlpin plantation that these women, taking the course indicated, could have run in a straight line to the tangled undergrowth of the bottom lands and then strike a small gulch having precipitous banks, several feet higher than their heads. The water in the bottom of this little gulch would have rendered it impossible for the dogs to follow their trail from the point where they had entered it, and following it back toward home they could have entered the shallow bayou between high cut banks at the junction, and then they could have walked up the bayou to a point not more than thirty yards from the back door of the McAlpin mansion. This, it will be remembered, tallies so accurately with Mrs. Stowe's story of the flight of Cassey and Emeline, that it seems impossible that she could have framed the story without an intimate knowledge of the peculiar topography of the McAlpin property.

Another very pronounced feature of similarity between the McAlpin estate of reality and the Legree plantation of the romance is found in the fact that the former is, and necessarily has been always isolated from neighboring plantations. On the southwest lie swamps and marshy lakes, bordered by rugged, thickly wood spurs from the rough hill country that reaches away westward, while the swampy bottoms of Cane river and its sluggish tributary and estuary bayous shut it in on the opposite boundary. In McAlpin's time the trails were few, tortuous, rough and very badly kept. McAlpin was the only white man resident on the place, so that had he willed it he might, with comparative safety, have enacted all the horrible barbarities which Mrs. Stowe's highly colored romance has attributed to him.

TRADITIONS OF ROBERT MCALPIN.

While it is practically impossible to believe that the story of Simon Legree is not a grossly exaggerated one, it must be admitted that it very accurately corresponds with the traditions that have been handed down as authentic history among the old negroes and the poorer classes of white settlers on Cane river concerning Robert McAlpin.

Still another point of resemblance between McAlpin and Legree is that while Mrs. Stowe declares Legree to have been a New Englander, the records show that after McAlpin's death the proceeds of the sale of his plantation and other property were remitted to his heirs, who were resident in New England.

In the forty-second chapter of "Uncle Tom's Cabin," which· follows Uncle Tom's death and burial, Mrs. Stowe says:

For some reason, ghostly legends were uncommonly rife about this time among the servants on Legree's place.

*   *   *   *   *   *

Authorities were somewhat divided as to the outward form of the spirit, owing to a custom quite prevalent among negroes, and for aught we know, among whites, too, of invariably shutting the eyes and covering up heads under blankets, petticoats, or whatever might come in use for a shelter on these occasions. Of course, as everybody knows, when the bodily eyes are thus out of the lists, the spiritual eyes are uncommonly vivacious and perspicuous, and therefore there were abundance of full-length portraits of the ghost abundantly sworn and testified to, which, as is often the case with portraits, agreed with each other in no particular except the common family peculiarity of the ghost tribe—the wearing of a white sheet.

*   *   *   *   *   *

Be it as it may, we have private reasons for knowing that a tall figure in a white sheet did walk, at the most approved ghostly hours, around the Legree premises—pass out the doors, glide about the house— disappear at intervals, and reappearing, pass up the silent stairway into that fatal garret; and that, in the morning, the entry doors were all found shut and locked as firm as ever.

Legree could not help overhearing this whispering, and it was all the more exciting to him, from the pains that were taken to conceal it from him. He drank more brandy than usual, held up his head briskly, and swore louder than ever in the daytime; but he had bad dreams, and the visions of his head on his bed were anything but agreeable. The night after Tom's body had been carried away he rode to the next town for a carouse, and had a high one. Got home late and tired, locked his door, took out the key and went to bed.

*   *   *   *   *   *   *

LEGREE'S DEATH.

But Legree locked his doors and set a chair against it; he set a night lamp at the head of his bed, and he put his pistols there. He examined the catches and fastenings of the windows and then swore he "didn't care for the devil and all his angels," and went to sleep.

Well, he slept, for he was tired—slept soundly.

But finally there came over his sleep a shadow, a horror, an apprehension of something hanging over him. It was his mother's shroud, he thought, but Cassey had it holding it up, and showing it to him. He had heard a confused noise of screams and groanings; and, with it all, he knew he was asleep, and he struggled to wake himself. He was half awake. He was sure something was coming into his room. He knew the door was opening, but he could not stir hand nor foot. At last he turned, with a start; the door was open, and he saw a hand putting out his light.

It was a cloudy, misty moonlight, and there he saw it!—something white, gliding in! He heard the still rustle of its ghostly garments. It stood still by his bed, a cold hand touched his; a voice said, three times in a low, fearful whisper, "Come! come! come!" And, while he lay sweating with terror, he knew not when or how, the thing was gone. He sprang out of bed and pulled at the door. It was shut and locked, and the man fell down in a swoon.

After this Legree became a harder drinker than ever before. He no longer drank cautiously, prudently, but imprudently and recklessly. There were reports around the country, soon after, that he was sick and dying. Excess had brought on that frightful disease that seems to throw the lurid shadows of a coming retribution back into the present life. None could bear the horrors of that sick-room when he raved and screamed, and spoke of sights which almost stopped the blood of those who heard him; and, at his dying-bed stood a stern, white, inexorable figure, saying, "Come! come! come!"

Such is the story of the tragic ending of Simon Legree, as told by Mrs. Stowe.

DEDUCTIONS DRAWN.

It has already been pointed out as a proof of Robert McAlpin's reputation for cruelty that there have been stories of his ghost haunting the plantation and the old mansion ever since he died. Is anything more probable than that these ghost stories may have had their origin in something very like the stories just quoted from Mrs. Stowe's novel? How much retailing of traditions among ignorant and superstitious negroes would it take to transfer the identity of a ghost from one of McAlpin's numerous victims to McAlpin himself?

Mrs. Stowe has luridly painted Simon Legree's last hours in the foregoing quotation. Cane river traditions agree in saying that Robert McAlpin died of mania potu.

It may be, indeed it is probable, that Robert McAlpin was not as black as tradition has painted him, and it is highly probable that no slaveholder in Louisiana ever practiced such atrocities as those which Mrs. Stowe has attributed to Simon Legree; but that Mrs. Stowe could have written the story of Simon Legree and his plantation without an intimate knowledge of the McAlpin mansion and plantation, as well as the stories that have now passed into tradition concerning McAlpin, is about as probable as that one could shake up a bushel of letters in a bag and then, blindfold, pour them out of the bag in such order as to spell the Lord's prayer. Theoretically, such a feat is not impossible, but the chances are millions to one against it. This letter makes no claim for the accuracy of Mrs. Stowe's pictures of slavery times, but it does claim that she had Robert McAlpin and his place in mind when she penned her chapters about Simon Legree and his plantation, and, therefore, that the cabin which Mr. Corley is about to ship to Chicago is an historic relic in that it is without doubt the veritable cabin in which the prototype of Mrs. Stowe's hero lived when on the plantation of the planter whom she has called Simon Legree.

A VISTA OF THE PAST.

I had been reading those chapters of "Uncle Tom's Cabin" relating to Simon Legree until a late hour the night before I landed here, and possibly this had caused me to be exceptionally impressionable as I found myself hurriedly dropped upon the supposed scene of that tragic romance but half awake, and before daybreak; but be that as it may, as I stood upon the little station platform and watched the gray dawn of a dull damp morning in late autumn stealing over the sombre levels of bottom land, clothed with the dark brown furze of ripened and half denuded cotton-stalks and faded yellow corn-stalks here and there broken down and trodden into the brick-red soil, and while I traced the dark outlines of the wooded hills slowly breaking through the cold steely mists that were drifting lazily upward into the low-hanging clouds, I could not but look for the tall and slender Cassey walking proudly and silently beside "Uncle Tom" in every group of negroes that were passing out toward the cotton fields. As the light grew stronger I readily recognized the Legree mansion from the novel's description, in a dark, grizzly old house with lofty gables just within the shadow of the wooded spur that runs from the far-off hills down to the verge of Cane river; and although of the row of cabins which had constituted the "quarters" but one remained upon its original site, it required no stretch of imagination to fix upon it as "Uncle Tom's," though others of a similar character were to be seen scattered in various directions about the plantation.

LEGREE'S GRAVE.

When the morning was well advanced, and the clouds had been banished by a flood of brilliant sunshine, I saw another relic of the old times, to which the novel makes no reference. Near the old mansion I had climbed up the slope of the thickly wooded spur to the crest of a little round-topped hill, which rises some fifty feet above the surrounding levels, and found myself in a strange old burying-ground. It was here that for many years all who died upon the plantation had been buried. There were no shrubs nor flowers, no grass-covered mounds, no graveled walks. The ground was thickly carpeted with dead and decaying leaves, the accumulations of generations; but beneath this thick carpet were swelling mounds on every side, and at the head and foot of many were rough stakes, weather-stained and crumbling into decay. The great sycamores, oaks and cottonwoods grew thickly all around, but they seemed to be falling into a decadence gruesomely suggestive of that solemn change that awaits everything that has life, sentient or insentient. The oak leaves were dyed with the deep purple and bronze of autumn, and there were leaves of gold and yellow and richest carmine still fluttering in the breezes that stirred the lighter branches of these old monarchs of the forest; but there were gnarled and rugged vines coiling themselves like grizzled, scaly serpents about their thick trunks, slowly but surely choking out their lives, and subtly drinking their heart's blood through slender, graceful tendrils of daintiest green. From the great limbs whose interlocking branches formed a rude canopy through which only here and there an errant ray of golden sunshine could find its way, hung broad streamers of Spanish moss like banners of sable crape, grown tattered, weather-stained and gray in their long and weary vigil over the forgotten and unheeded dead.

It was here that I saw the last resting-place of Robert McAlpin. It is the only grave of the many scattered over the hill that gives evidence of having been cared for. Four low walls of red brick rise a few inches out of the ground, and from these some time sprang a low-pitched arch or roof of the same material. Now the bricks are half crumbled away, and what remain are encrusted with dark green moss. The tomb has partially caved in, and in a few more years the ever-thickening carpet of dead leaves will have hidden it from view, leaving only a leaf-covered mound to mark the final resting-place of the rich and proud planter as he sleeps side by side with those who forty years ago were wont to know no higher law than his unbending will.

QUESTIONS.

What were the names of the Virgin Mary's parents?

What were the names of the two thieves who were crucified with the Savior? Which was on the right, and which on the left? Which one of the two did the Savior pardon?

When did Matthew write his Gospel? Where did Matthew die?

What was St. Peter's mother's name? What was his wife's name? Where did Peter die, and what was the manner of his death?

What was the manner of death that all of the apostles died?

Where was St. Andrew killed? Who had it done? Who had him buried? Who had his remains removed and reinterred?

Where was Mary Magdalene buried, and by whom was she buried? By whose order were her remains removed? To where, and when were they removed?

How long did the Virgin Mary live after the Crucifixion? By whom was she buried after her death?

What was the name of the Roman soldier who pierced the Savior's side with a spear?

What was Mrs. Pilate's given name? What was the name of the woman who was brought before the Savior on a charge of adultery? What became of her afterward?

What was the name of the Elect Lady to whom the Second Epistle of John was addressed? What position did she hold in the church?

Which one of the apostles was accompanied in his travels by his sister? What was that sister's name?

With what did Judas Iscariot hang himself? Upon what did he hang himself?

What did Josephus say about Jesus Christ? What did he say about one of Christ's apostles, and which one of the apostles was it? What did he say about John the Baptist? When was Josephus born? When did he die?

These and many other interesting questions are answered in

CORLEY'S LIVES OF THE TWELVE APOSTLES.

Hon. M. A. Spoonts, of Fort Worth, Texas, says: "The examination that I have given your 'Lives of the Apostles' has led me to believe that the religious world is very much your debtor for having brought so much valuable information, thought and judgment, on a subject of which so little is known, within the reach of the most humble person.

"The little volume is a store-house of religious knowledge, and should be in the hands of every family; and if some of the money ordinarily wasted on pernicious books, or for periodicals of doubtful value, was spent for this good book, the moral life of the young of the land would be greatly elevated. The price, $1.00, is much less than the cost of the ordinary newspaper, and when the relative value of each is considered, it is hard to understand how any person can hesitate to invest in it, and afterward spend their money for some frivolous periodical. If you will place the merits of the book before the Christian people, I predict for it a large sale."

Rev. John Duke McFaden, manager of "The Brethren Tract Society," of Philadelphia, and author of "The Story of Jesus," a little book so popular that one young lady has already sold 17,000 copies, says: "Your book, 'Lives of the Apostles,' is as valuable as interesting, and that is saying much. Every Sunday-school library should have one or more copies. I no longer believe the disciples were cowardly. Your book has changed several assertions, so it has done good already. I have spoken of it to my friends and will give it a good notice in my paper. It deserves a wide circulation. May God bless your work."

Rev. A. S. Bunting, pastor Cisco Baptist church, Cisco, Texas, says: "I have read this book with a good degree of interest and pleasure. The writer exhibits a degree of fairness and candor in sifting testimony that is not always found in presenting some of the character sketches found in this book. It is rather unique in some positions taken, which indicates the author as an independent thinker. I cheerfully recommend it to all as a book worthy of a careful reading."

Hon. T. H. Conner, judge of the 42d judicial district of Texas, says: "I have read with much interest your 'Lives of the Twelve Apostles.' All that pertains to the 'witnesses' upon whose testimony we so largely rely in our faith in the Great Redeemer of mankind will ever be of profound interest. Your book contains much valuable information that is unattainable by the average reader, and I very cheerfully recommend it to all those interested in the Bible and in the problem of eternal life."

www.ingramcontent.com/pod-product-compliance
Lightning Source LLC
Chambersburg PA
CBHW030009030726
47499CB00008B/2968